To Cousin Fallon, and all the caregivers
who carry the load, lovingly so
TC

To my parents, Ylda and Esau;
my brother, Pepe; and my husband, Ed
SP

Text copyright © 2021 by Tami Charles
Illustrations copyright © 2021 by Sara Palacios

First edition 2021

Library of Congress Catalog Card Number pending
ISBN 978-0-7636-9749-5

20 21 22 23 24 25 LEO 10 9 8 7 6 5 4 3 2 1

Printed in Heshan, Guangdong, China

This book was typeset in Burbank.
The illustrations were done in gouache
and assembled digitally.

Candlewick Press
99 Dover Street
Somerville, Massachusetts 02144

www.candlewick.com

MY DAY WITH THE PANYE

Tami Charles

illustrated by Sara Palacios

CANDLEWICK PRESS

In the hills of Port-au-Prince, Manman's voice, sweet like mango, sings to the sky.

"Fallon," she calls. "Would you like to go to market with me?"

"Yes!" I say.

My little sister, Naima, cries, "Me too!"

"Another time, pitit. Your day will come, but today it's Fallon's turn."

Manman wraps her hair in a silk mouchwa, brighter than the Caribbean sea.

I twist my sun-yellow scarf into my braids, but it doesn't look as good as hers.

Manman tightens my mouchwa.

Then she places the panye on her head.

More than anything—more than I want to wear the finest silk
in Haiti—I want to carry the basket like Manman does.

"May I try?"

"Slowly," Manman says.

My toes start to prickle.

I dash for the door.

BOOM!

The panye falls and crashes to the floor.

Manman takes up the panye, and we start on our trip.

"Bye-bye, Naima. Bye-bye, Grann. See you soon."

Manman says, "When I was your age, my manman would say, 'Pitit, pitit, zwazo fe nich li.' *Little by little the bird builds its nest.* Not everything is learned fast."

My heart sinks like a shooting star in the midnight sky. If only Manman would give me one more try.

On our walk to market, Manman is tall like an arrow pointing to the clouds. Her hips sway, but the panye doesn't move.

"Look around, Fallon. Our neighborhood will show you the way."

The tap-tap bus chug-a-lugs by, carrying people with sun-beaten faces full of laughter louder than a rooster's crow. Kompa music echoes through the wind.

"To carry the panye, we move gracefully, even under the weight of the sun and the moon."

But more than riding the tap-tap, heavy with happy people, more than moving to the kompa rhythms, I just want to carry the panye.

"May I try again?"

"Pitit, pitit, not just yet. Pitit, pitit, build your nest."

We walk past colorful walls—swirls of blue like a cloudless sky, green and red like the coffee plants sprouting at our feet.

"To carry the panye is to be strong. Even after the earthquake shook Haiti to pieces, these walls still stand."

"Like the panye stays still on your head?"

Manman claps. "That's it!"

But more than the colorful walls, still standing, painted blue, green, and red, I want to grab the panye, place it high on my head.

"May I try now?"

"Pitit, pitit. Almost there."

We reach the market, and there's food everywhere: sacks of potatoes, round like the moon; fat pumpkins, yellow-orange like the sun.

"Famille!" Cousin Yolene sings out. She owns the vegetable stand.

Manman pulls out some gourdes to pay Cousin for our food. Into the panye our dinner goes.

I see mothers and daughters, walking like they have gold in their shoes.

Their feet are graceful. Their panyes are still, even as the wind swirls through the city.

Manman holds my hand. "To carry the panye is—"

"To care for our family?" I say.

Manman smiles banana-wide.

The sun dances across the sky. The tap-tap chug-a-lugs by. Women pack their goods, close their shops, and we begin our walk home.

"Manman, more than the sun and all the stars far away, I'm ready to carry the panye."

Manman stares me down with honey-brown eyes.

"Isit. Here." She helps me with the mouchwa and then places the panye on my head, so heavy I can barely stand.

The panye wobbles . . .

bobbles . . .

and crashes to the ground.
Vegetables fly everywhere!

My heart sinks like a shooting star.
I do not want to give it another try.
But Manman will not hear it.

"It's OK, Fallon," she says as she helps
me load the panye again.

"Pitit, pitit, build your nest." Manman
returns the heavy basket to my head.

With my back like an arrow,
I take one step,
        another,
                and another.
Not too fast.
Little by little.

I feel myself stretch to the clouds. I walk like a queen. I walk like Manman . . . all the way home.

The sun kisses the moon bon soir as we reach the door.

"What does the panye mean to you, Fallon?"

With my feet planted in the cool sand, I say, "The panye means we are graceful when the load is heavy. We are strong, even when the earth is not. We are family, fed from love."

"Le bon. That is good."

The door swings open.

"My turn!" Naima jumps for the panye.

"Pitit, pitit, build your nest," I say.

"What nest? I'm not a bird!"

Manman and I sing in laughter to the blue-gray sky.

"Oh, little sister, I will show you. Soon you'll have your day."

AUTHOR'S NOTE

The act of carrying a panye, or basket, on the head dates back to ancient times and is still practiced in many parts of the world, such as Africa, South Asia, the Middle East, and the Caribbean. Though these baskets are generally carried by women and girls, boys and young men carry loads this way sometimes as well.

The basket can hold important items like food, clothes, and even firewood. Carrying the panye is a skill taught at an early age, which is why by adulthood many carriers walk with ease, even though the load may be heavy.

Walking with the panye is a cheaper way of transporting goods than using a vehicle like this story's tap-tap, which is a bus that you pay to ride on.

My Day with the Panye focuses on my husband's homeland of Haiti—an island with a rich history of triumph. Haiti is the world's first Black republic and the first independent Caribbean nation after European colonization.

Haiti is a beautiful place, which is why I wrote this story. But a lot of sad events have occurred there, such as the decimation of the indigenous population, the struggle for independence following three hundred years of slavery on the island, and a devastating earthquake in 2010 that claimed more than 200,000 lives.

Pride, love, and joy still shine through on the island and in its people at home and abroad. You can see it in the markets, where many women proudly run their own businesses. You can feel it in the music, the food, and in the walls that remain and stand tall today.